"She is worth far more than rubies. Her children arise and call her blessed. Honor her for all that her hands have done."

—Proverbs 31: 10, 28, 31

ONDERKIDZ

e Berenstain Bears® Mother's Day Blessings

opyright © 2016 by Berenstain Publishing, Inc.
ustrations © 2016 by Berenstain Publishing, Inc.

is book is also available as a Zondervan ebook.
sit www.zondervan/ebooks.

quests for information should be addressed to:

nderkidz, 3900 Sparks Dr. SE, Grand Rapids, Michigan 49546

BN 978-0-310-74869-4

Scripture quotations, unless otherwise indicated, are taken from The Holy
ole, *New International Version*®, *NIV*®. Copyright © 1973, 1978, 1984, 2011 by
olica, Inc.® Used by permission. All rights reserved worldwide.

itor: Mary Hassinger
t direction: Cindy Davis

nted in China

16 17 18 /LPC/ 12 11 10 9 8 7 6 5 4 3 2 1

By Mike Berenstain
Based on the characters created by
Stan & Jan Berenstain

It was spring in Bear Country and Mother's Day was not far off. Scenes of motherhood were all around—a mother deer and her fawn, a mother bluebird and her chicks, a mother woodchuck showing her kits how to munch dandelions.

Brother, Sister, and Honey Bear were thinking about Mother's Day. They wanted to surprise Mama with something very special on her big day. But they were having trouble coming up with something special enough. So, they went to Papa for help.

"Well," said Papa, when he heard their problem, "a Sunday brunch at the Bear Country Inn would be nice. That's Mama's favorite place to eat."

"Great!" said Sister. "And we could invite Grizzly Gran too. Then it would be a double Mother's Day surprise!"

"Good idea," said Brother. "We could go right after church on Sunday morning."

They could hardly wait for Mother's Day to arrive so they could surprise both Mama and Grizzly Gran.

When Mother's Day morning finally dawned, the cubs dashed into Mama and Papa's room and jumped on the bed.

"Happy Mother's Day!" they cried.

"We have a surprise for you but we don't want to tell you yet!" said Sister.

"Oh?" said Mama.

"We'll tell you after church," said Brother. "You'll love it!"

"Thank you, my dears!" said Mama, giving them big hugs and kisses. "You certainly are wonderful cubs."

"And you are the most wonderful-est mother in the whole, wide world!" said Sister, hugging her back.

"Yes!" agreed Brother making it a group hug by bringing Honey in for the snuggle too. "And the most special-est, too!"

"Special!" said Honey, hugging for all she was worth.

Before long, the Bear family was on their way to church. They saw other families going places with their moms too.

"Everyone is out and about," said Mama, smiling. "Mother's Day certainly is nice for us moms. Did you ever stop to think that children everywhere think their own mothers are the most special mothers of all?"

The cubs looked at each other. They couldn't say they had.

Soon they were driving past Officer Marguerite directing traffic.

"Officer Marguerite has to work on Mother's Day," said Mama. "But look, her children are bringing her flowers to make her Mother's Day extra-special."

"Wow!" said the cubs.

"It seems Dr. Gert Grizzly is working today too," said Mama, nodding toward the hospital entrance. "And so arc other hospital moms. Their families are bringing them right there—Mother's Day presents, cards, and all."

"Gee!" said Sister. "I didn't even know Dr. Grizzly was a mother."

"Me, neither," said Brother. "I just thought she was a doctor."

Mama laughed. "Doctors, nurses, police officers, emergency crews—and homemakers like me—we can all be mothers."

"Look, there!" said Papa as they drove past Farmer Ben's farm. "Moms can be farmers too—like Mrs. Ben."

"Mother's Day or no Mother's Day, farm work needs to be done every day of the year," said Mama. "So Mrs. Ben is hard at work as usual. But her sons and daughters are right there with her, showing how much they love her."

Next the Bear family drove past the junkyard.

"It looks like the Grizzly family is closing up the junkyard for Mother's Day," said Mama. "There's the whole clan—Two-Ton, their father, Too-Much, their daughter, and their son Too-Tall—all taking their mother, Too-Too, to church."

When the Bear family arrived at the Chapel in the Woods, they greeted friends and neighbors.

"Hello, Mrs. Grizzle!" said the cubs to their regular babysitter. She was arm-in-arm with a very large bear. Brother and Sister had never seen him before.

"Hello, cubs," said Mrs. Grizzle. "Meet my son, Zed. He's visiting from out of town for Mother's Day."

"Pleased t' meet ya," growled Zed, shaking hands. His paws were huge. He took off his hat. "Happy Mother's Day, Mrs. Bear," he said to Mama.

"Why, thank you, Zed!" said Mama taking his other arm as they went into church.

They were greeted at the door by Mrs. Brown, the preacher's wife. Her grown son and daughter were there, too, handing out programs.

"Mrs. Brown does so much for the church," said Mama. "Sometimes I think she works harder than Preacher Brown, himself."

"It's a shame she has to work on Mother's Day," said Sister.

"Yes," said Mama. "But her children are here for her. And that's what's most important to us moms—to have our children around us."

Inside the chapel, the Bears went to their usual pew and sat with Grizzly Gran and Gramps.

"Happy Mother's Day, Gran!" said the cubs. "We have a special Mother's Day surprise for you and Mama!"

"Is that so, grand cubs?" said Gran, winking at Papa. She already knew all about it. "Well, let's don't spoil the surprise. It'll wait until after church."

And they all settled down for the service.

"Welcome!" began Preacher Brown. "Special Mother's Day blessings to all the mothers here and everywhere in Bear Country. On this day we give thanks to God for all of you—and for what each of you has done for us—for feeding and caring for us, for guiding our feet in the paths of the Lord, and for raising us to be good, strong, and healthy.

As the Bible says,
'Your mother was like a vine in your vineyard
planted by the water; it was fruitful and full of branches.'"

The cubs imagined Mama sprouting leaves and branches. It made
them giggle.
"Hush!" said Mama.
They hushed.

"Now, what's this Mother's Day surprise you're itchin' to tell me about?" asked Gran after the service.

"We're taking you and Mama to brunch at the Bear Country Inn!" said the cubs.

"A good thing too," said Gran. "I'm half starved!"

"Me too!" said Mama.

"Better feed 'em, quick," said Gramps, "or they'll get cranky!"

"Really, Gramps," said Gran.

And they drove away through the beautiful Bear Country spring morning and a happy Mother's Day was had by all.